PSYCHE
Find your own Reality

Novel by

TORRE ODELL

Duke Publishing

Duke Publishing

Duke.Publishing1@gmail.com

The characters and events in this book are fictitious. Any similarity to real persons, living or dead, is coincidental and not intended by the author.

Printed in the United States of America

Library of Congress Catalog-in-Publication Data

Odell, Torre

Psyche: a novel / Torre Odell

ISBN: 0615514774
ISBN-13: 9780615514772

ACKNOWLEDGEMENTS

I would like to thank my friends and family for their love and support. I'd also like to thank Duke Publishing for this opportunity.

CONTENTS

Acknowledgments

PSYCHE

Find your own Reality

1

INTRODUCTION

I wake up feeling sicker than I have ever felt before, like after a long night of binge drinking. My body feels beaten and my eyes carry images across the room. Everything blurs from object to object and it only exacerbates my nausea. My shirt is lightly bouncing off my chest due to the hard pumps from my heart. I feel every beat pulsate through my head. I pull in half a breath then my chest collapses. The voices in my head are louder than normal; they won't stop. My skull is throbbing as I put my moist palms on my head. I can feel the cooling sweat against my hot skin. My eyes water as I turn over in my bed and glance at the clock, 8:00am on the dot. I feel so weak; I pull myself to my feet and almost fall back on the bed but catch myself on the bed post. My legs quiver like wet noodles; soreness and infirmity flood my body in an unrelenting manner. There is no medicine for what I have.

Today everything is dark, not dim or faint, just dark. Unlike the past few days when the world had more life and color, now it's bland and unnervingly motionless. I slowly stumble into the closet. There's an antique case on the top shelf next to my gym bag. This case is the only thing in the closet my eyes can focus on. I extend my arms and pull the case down. I take a deep breath as I open it to see the 9mm that was given to me by my uncle on my last birthday. I look at it for a moment and stare at my reflection bouncing off the smooth silver finish. My blue eyes seem to burn into the steel. I grab the clip and slide it in, the cold steel is a comfort in my hands. I push in the clip and hear the click whisper "it's okay" lightly into my ear; I take another deep breath as I slowly slide a round into the chamber. I do it slowly so I can watch the bullet move into position before I slide the top back into place. I walk through the hallway and into the living room. I notice only static items that clutter my house. The family portraits are blank. The picture frames hold images my mind won't allow my eyes focus on. I sit on the couch and lean back, whimpering with pain and anger.

Tunnel vision and distant memories flood my consciousness. Old memories that I wish I could relive start tormenting me. My chest begins to constrict causing a chain reaction of pain that darts down my body as the voices in my head get louder and more prominent. They're driving me mad! Thunderous words that I can't make out. All I get from them are mind splitting headaches that irritate every fiber of my being. All my thoughts and memories begin to blend together and nothing makes sense anymore. Every word that chimes in my head cause my vision to shake and shutter. I can't move past this and it just keeps getting worse. My world is falling apart; my very fabric of existence is deteriorating with every moment I live. I don't want an easy way out. I'm a soldier, a husband, a father, and a friend to a world that's left me behind. A world that's given up on me; how things got so bad so quickly, I can't explain. I look down at the gun and admire the silvery finish as it begins to calm me again. I unwillingly pull the gun under my chin and I feel a tear roll down my left cheek as my head follows it down to the floor. The room begins to spin around me. My vision blurs and everything begins to fade away. Total silence enters the room and into my head. The relief is only temporary. The voices return and they've grown stronger than ever. They are yelling at me, but why? Why doesn't the torment end? Like clockwork the constrictions tear through me and shiver down my spine. Like chills from being cold but they brought a fire that flows through my veins and throughout my body. My body quivers in pain as I move my head up; I'm out of my home now and see my daughter running towards me smiling with my beautiful wife close behind her. She's running in a meadow pushing through the grass and bright yellow daises. She smiles at me as the sun reflects off her perfect little face. Her little hazel eyes are the sharpest colors in this memory. I barely feel the tears as they continue to roll down my face while I come to terms with the fact that this unclear, but understandable image, will be the last time I see them, my girls, the loves of my life. How do you fall asleep and wake up to such a twisted hell? A place where everyone and everything plays tricks on you, a place where you can't trust anything you see, think, or feel. A twilight zone so surreal you feel like you've awakened in a dream that's actually a reality. I will never kill myself; I've said it a million times throughout life. Suicide is never the right answer to any question life brings. My thoughts deepen as I envision kneeling down and hugging my daughter. My wife smiles and places her arms around us. This to me won't be suicide; it'll be a release. I slide my finger onto the trigger and start to squeeze. I can hear the hammer pull back, the light squeaks whisper "it's okay" and my ears focus on that sound. Then the hammer slams back into the gun. The room jumps quickly, and then everything goes black.

2

STORY BEGINS

I wake up early on a Sunday morning and it feels like any other morning. The only significant difference today is that I'm taking my wife and daughter to the zoo. My wife Marie and I have been several times but it will be our four-year old daughter Katie's first. She loves animals, not unlike any other four-year old I could imagine. This is exceedingly obvious by simply walking into her room which has been ambushed by wildlife posters and stuffed animals. I lean up and put my feet on the ground and head toward the kitchen to get a bottle of water. I see clothes and toys all over the floor so my wife and daughter must already be awake. I start searching the apartment and find them together in the bathroom.

"Honey, are you in there?" I ask as I slowly open the bathroom door.

"Cory, I'm getting Katie out of the bath give me a second, please."

"Can I come in? Everyone descent?"

"Yes, it's okay."

I walk into the bathroom and see my wife drying off Katie. My daughter looks up at me while she sings about going bye, bye.

"Hey, before we go to the zoo can we stop at Wal-Mart to get a shower curtain? I'm tired of taking baths." My wife asks as she tries to control our playful daughter.

"That's fine with me, I honestly feel the same way. I still can't believe the last one tore so easily." I reply as I make funny faces towards Katie.

"Also, just so you know, I moved the gun you received for your birthday last year from the dining room mantle. I was scared Katie would pull out a chair and get it down. Just trying to be safe".

"Ok, that's probably for the best, where did you put it?"

"I put it in our closet on the top shelf by your gym bag."

"Cool. I guess we'll grab something to eat after we hit up Wal-Mart on the way to the zoo."

Katie hears the word zoo and starts screaming. "Lions and tigers and bears! I want to see a cheetah!"

"Baby calm down, we'll be there soon enough ok." Marie tells Katie while they both laugh as she tries to calm her down and dry her off.

After what seemed like an eternity of preparation we head out. As we leave our apartment I notice how amazing the day is, the sun's shining bright and the sky is clear with no clouds in sight. The air is filled with the sweet fragrance of flowers. It's funny how normally you see flowers but you never smell them in the air, but today it was definitely apparent.

During the drive my wife and I discuss whether or not we're going to stay in the military. We were lucky enough to meet while stationed in Abilene together but it might not be beneficial for the future. The military life can be detrimental to a relationship and a family due to its instability and stress.

We pull into the crowded parking lot outside of Wal-Mart and luckily find a spot near the entrance. I get out of my truck and open my daughter's door and begin to remove her from her car seat. As I put her on the ground she begins to sing "*twinkle, twinkle little star*" and asks if I'll sing along with her.

"Not right now baby, if Daddy sings that song you might not like it anymore."

"Cory, you're horrible, why don't you sing with her?" Marie asks while she smirks at me.

"I just like hearing her sing, that's all. Plus I've never really been the singing in public type. I'll keep that in the shower where it belongs."

"Sure." Marie replies with a smile.

We walk toward the store as Katie jumps up and down with every beat in her song.

As we come up on the cross walk in front of the store, I hear a car screeching around the corner of the parking lot with their music blaring. I pull my wife and daughter close to me as I back them up. We wait to see what this car was going to do. I hold my daughter's hand and look down at her to make sure she's behind me but then a women lets out a horrific scream.

"No, Kristen stop!"

I quickly pull my head up to find the commotion. I see a little girl wearing a light-blue sun dress walking into the road while looking down at a game. I turn back towards the car and its speeding towards her. Without thinking I push Katie and Marie back and dart into the street. I feel my wife grab my arm to try and stop me but I quickly pull away.

I hear her voice as she screams at the back of my head "Wait Cory!"

But I'm not thinking, just reacting. I move as fast as I can and I stretch my arms out towards the little girl; the world seems to slow down except for the speeding car that I start to see out of my peripheral vision. My fingers just barely touch the little girl's light-blue dress as I feel the heat from the car accompanied by hard rock music inch closer and closer. As my finger tips start to feel the fabric of her dress I begin to push as hard as I can, then I feel a quick jolt. The smell of burning rubber and hot air press firmly against my face and pain shoots into my body. I start seeing quick flashes of everything around me as the concrete starts tearing my flesh off from my body. When my body stops rolling and starts slowing down I start to feel the pain and dizziness set in. People are running all around as the concrete starts to heat up my face; the little girl disappears from my mind as I feel my body slide across the parking lot in front of the store. I'm lying on my stomach and I can't move. I keep trying to get up but I can't and my eyes begin to roll back into my head. The hot concrete burns my face and I see blood gathering in front my eyes.

My eyes begin opening erratically and my hearing seems to come and go. I start seeing and hearing things in short flashes. My mind starts to split as the sounds of sirens enter the air. My eyes become hard to open as they start sealing from the blood gathering on them.

The ambulance constantly shakes and feels out of control. I try to avoid the paramedics, especially their facial expressions which aren't very comforting. I see only looks of frantic emotion and annoyance. It matched the words that came out of their mouths too fast to even try to make sense of. My eyes won't focus on anything, they just run around the small area I found myself trapped in. My mind is flying in so many directions, was I ok? Was the little girl ok? Where was I hit? Where is my family? All these questions run rampant through my mind.

I was losing my nerves being surrounded by strangers and not knowing what was going on. The annoying breathing mask was scratching my face and it stopped the blood right below my eyes until it was full enough to spill into them. The blood felt thick and it was hard to see through. I try to fight off the paramedics and ask for answers then I see my wife and freeze. She was with me, holding my left hand, her eyes watering and tears rolling down her face as she stared at me. It was hard to hold my head up to see her, it felt so heavy and was just bobbing around. I laid it on my shoulder and just looked at her. I almost busted into tears myself when I realized she was holding my hand but I couldn't feel it. The paramedics kept trying to make me place my neck back into a mold for stabilization but I didn't want to. I wanted to see my wife not the ceiling of an ambulance.

I tried to squeeze my wife's hand but I couldn't. I wasn't able to move a finger on that hand or my arm either. I kept telling myself to calm down and that I had to pull myself back together and show some form of strength so Marie would feel more at ease and trust that I was fine and would be okay. The paramedics kept getting in my way asking me questions but I couldn't understand them. I was too focused on Marie, everything else I began to zone out. Seeing my wife was the only thing that made me feel better, it calmed me even with her tears. I felt safer knowing she was with me. I kept trying to talk through this dreadful mask to tell her it was going to be ok and that I loved her but I couldn't speak, the words couldn't find my lips. I couldn't get any sounds to get past the mask or over the commotion within the ambulance. Every time I tried to talk my body constricted and caused me even more pain. I couldn't pin point where all the pain was coming from, it just kept spreading all over my body. My chest felt sore but I couldn't feel any of my extremities that well and some not at all. My anger started to grow because the air mask was driving me crazy. I tried to avoid it as I looked at Marie; it felt like I was staring into her eyes for an eternity, an eternity that wouldn't be long enough. But they were just flashes. The paramedics forced my head down finally strapping it into the cushion. Now I was immobilized and I couldn't see my wife anymore. I tried to fight them off and turn back to her but I couldn't, I didn't know if she had my hand or not anymore and fear started setting in more and more. They began cutting off my shirt. Then I saw one reach over and pull my hand out of my wife's, I noticed because she wouldn't let go. I kept trying to stretch out to her but I couldn't. A paramedic put his face in front of mine and started talking to me. I couldn't make out his words or focus on him. He started yelling at me which became even more unnerving. They start strapping my arms and legs down. All I could move on my own were my eyes and they didn't cooperate most of the time. The male paramedic finally got out of my face and as he moved I noticed a female paramedic starting to rub two white paddles together. My body starts getting cold and I begin to shiver as fear engulfs me and squeezes me tighter. My hearing begins to come back but what I hear is a steady dull tone. They lower the paddles to my chest but I can't feel them. Everyone leans back as my body jumps; I feel extreme pain flow throughout my body starting in my chest. I constrict and my chest pulls my body off the gurney. I feel like I just caught on fire and the burning won't stop. Sounds quickly come back into my head as the noise of the ambulance is more present than before. I'm too terrified to focus on any one thing but I over hear the words "Re-charge the defibrillator; we need to shock him again."

I try to yell: "No, please stop it hurts!"

But I can't get the words to come out, I continue screaming the words in my head, but nothing. They put the paddles back on my chest and as the pain shoots back through me, my eyes widen and the noises fade away into silence.

3

AWAKENING

As my eyes begin to open a dull white ceiling starts coming into focus. Piercing florescent lights litter the ceiling. Then a vexing odor enters my nostrils and the smell is unmistakable. I knew without even looking around that I was in a hospital. I slowly turn my head and see Marie in the room talking with a doctor near the door. She looked beautiful as always, she's wearing her hair down, that always looks stunning on her. She doesn't seem as upset or scared anymore which is extremely comforting. I slowly start to lean up and turn to lower my feet to the floor. As my toes come in contact with the floor they curl back due to the icy surface. I rolled my neck to give it a little stretch, my body felt so tight like I was still pinned down. All my muscles felt exhausted like I just finished running a marathon. I look down to notice I'm wearing one of the ever revealing patient gowns, pea green with my ass out; great look for anyone. Marie sees me start to get out of bed and rushes over and wraps her arms around me. I breathe her in deeply and get lost in her sweet scent.

"Don't you ever do that to me again!" Marie whispers into my ear as she squeezes me tighter, I can't help but too smile.

"I promise baby. I didn't mean to scare you, I just acted. There wasn't much of a thought process that led me to that decision."

The doctor approaches and shakes my hand as he pulls out his little flash light.

"How are you feeling Cory? I'm Dr. Jones just try and follow the light with your eyes as best you can." He scans the light back and forth.

"Umm… I'm okay I think, I mean I feel tired and sore but otherwise I think I'm fine. I assumed I'd feel a lot worse." I respond while looking myself up and down.

He looks down at his clipboard: "Well you were lucky… you took quite a hit. But after the testing, MRI and x-rays I think you should be fine. You just need to get some rest."

The weird thing was I felt totally relaxed. I was sore and stiff but otherwise fine. There was no real pain anywhere which was weird remembering how I felt when it happened and what I saw in the ambulance.

I looked at Marie; "I'm sorry for scaring you, I didn't think…I just wanted to help."

"It's okay. You did scare me but I'm just glad your fine." She replies with teary eyes and a smile. I take her into my arms again and kiss her gently.

"Where is Katie… is she okay?" I ask as I look around the room.

"She's fine, I have a friend from work watching her."

"Oh, ok. That's good." I reply as I stand up and move towards the sink to look in the mirror.

I expect to see lacerations and bruises all over my face and body but surprisingly, there were no real bruises or anything. No lacerations or cuts. An astonished look comes over my face. I looked like I did before the accident, except for my new little stylish outfit. I turned to the doctor with a bewildered look.

I almost stutter while I ask, "Doc, why don't I have any bruises or real pain? Especially for what seemed to be so serious of an accident? I mean I remember getting hit by a car and seeing blood. How come I look fine? You even said I was lucky and I was transported here in an ambulance."

He takes his glasses off and lowers his clip board as his eyes meet mine.

"Well, like I said before, you were lucky. We gave you drugs to numb the pain so they are probably still working in your system now. That's why there's no constant pain. As for no bruises or lacerations that's just because there are none. Sometimes your mind makes situations worse then they may actually be."

I raise an eyebrow at him as I can't help but to smirk; "I felt a damn car hit me, I saw blood coming down my head and on my body. I watched them tear my shirt off and shock me with those little paddle things. You say I have no pain due to the drugs, ok I'll buy that. But what did you give me to make me look normal?" I ask with a sarcastic and upset underlying tone in my voice.

"My mind didn't trick me into believing I was in a worse condition then I actually was. I was there and I know what happened."

The doctor gives me a puzzled look like I asked a totally obscene question and statement. I turn to him again and ask, "Doc do you not understand what I'm asking?"

I stand up and walk towards him as I look over at Marie to see if she's at least on the same page as me but she looks lost as well. I turn back to Dr. Jones and lean in towards him. "I was hit by a car! I rode in an ambulance and I remember my wife having blood on her clothes and now there is no blood on her and none on me. There isn't even a stain on her shirt. Oh yea and I couldn't feel my legs and arms while riding here before I passed out. I remember being shocked twice with your paramedic's paddles. Now I wake up and you say I was lucky and I'm fine? My mind has been playing tricks on me. Not to be rude but what the shit man?"

The doctor looks over at Marie like I just figured out a huge secret that they were hiding from me. Then replies; "Look son, you're confused and tired. You need to just take a deep breath and calm down. You've been through a traumatic experience today and you need to focus on feeling better, okay. You just need some sleep. Things will make more sense to you then, okay?"

I take a deep breath to try and curb my anger. I raise my hand to my temples and start moving my fingers in small circular motions. "Okay, fine whatever but if I feel bad tomorrow or later tonight I'm going to come back up here and ask for you. If by tomorrow I still feel like something isn't right I'm coming back. Is that cool?"

"That would be fine and I hope you do if you start feeling bad again. I have no problem with that. You just need to try an relax."

On the drive home I just stare into the side view mirror looking for cuts or bruises but there are none to be found. The medicine must still be working because all of the colors on the buildings seem to blur into one another. My body feels light like I'm starting to drift away. My wife starts rubbing my shoulder and I turn to her and asked about the girl I pushed.

"She's fine. She has some bruises because of how hard you pushed her but that's all. She would've been killed if you hadn't helped her. The parents wanted me to thank you and apologize for them; they want to meet you soon. Oh and by the way, I already called the base and told them about what happened and they said to take the next couple days off to recuperate, they have the manning for you to miss a little work."

"That's good I'm not going to fight free days off and that's funny the little girl has bruises from me pushing her. I mean I was hit by a car and have no bruises."

She gives me an annoyed look that I must admit was quite unnerving.

"What about my supervisor? Did you already talk to him?"

"Yes, he said he'd talk to you in a few days. He said to just take it easy and if you need anything to call him".

"I have to feel out a safety report don't I?"

"Yes, but they said it's not a big rush. The verbal report I gave them was sufficient for now. You can do it in a couple days. A few people from work and our Commander came to visit you but you were still being looked at, once they heard you'd be fine they left and said they'd talk to you once you get back to work."

I leaned back in the car; "Ok, I just want to relax anyways. Besides you and Katie, I really don't want to see anyone."

As we turn down the street heading to our apartment, my eyes begin to go out of focus and my surroundings begin to seem bleak and quiet. I shake my head and look at my wife; "Did everything just get dimmer or am I going crazy?"

I ask while I laugh. My head starts to feel heavy and begins to bob.

"You've just had a long day baby don't worry."

"Don't you have to pick up Katie?"

"I let her stay at a Crystal's house, her daughter is throwing a little party so I thought that would be nice, plus I figured you'd want it to be quiet so you could rest. Katie was shaken up about everything so I thought it would be a nice way to take her mind off of everything."

"Aww, I wanted to see her especially after today…it's ok, I feel fine, a little woozy now but otherwise fine, I feel bad we didn't get to take her to the zoo. I know she was excited about that. We have to make that happen."

As we enter the apartment, I head straight towards my bedroom.

"I think I'm going to lie down, I'm exhausted. Do you want to tuck me in?"

"I'll be in there in a minute baby."

I enter the room and lie down; I gaze up at the ceiling and watch the fan blades circle over and over again until I fall asleep.

4

PAIN COMMENCES

I feel as if I wake up as quickly as I laid down, yet I feel refreshed; like I've slept for days. I lean up and look around the room and notice everything is dim, not only the light but the colors seem vague and unadorned. As I turn towards the clock I notice it is exactly eight o'clock. I don't remember even setting the alarm. Out of nowhere, my right arm begins to twitch then I get a pain in my right forearm directly where the arm bends; I look down and see blood start to roll out from in front of my elbow. There were no holes or cuts just blood oozing out. My hand starts to shake and gets colder; I start feeling a little freaked out so I jump out of bed and start looking for Marie. I walk out of the bedroom in just my boxers while holding my arm behind my elbow. I imagine this has to be a pathetic sight.

"Marie, are you here? Hello?"

There's no answer, I push the bathroom door open and it slams against the wall. I pull a white towel off the rack and wrap it around my arm.

"Marie? Hello? Are you home? What the hell." I yell again as my blood starts to boil.

Still no answer, maybe she went to work and just didn't check on me or tell me goodbye. That's nice of her. I walk over to the front door and notice her keys are missing from the holder on the wall. I pick up the phone and call the base.

"Command Post Tech Sergeant Hamilton, how may I help you?"

"Hey Tech Sergeant Hamilton its Cory, just curious have you seen Marie today?"

"No, I haven't seen her let me check the schedule. Actually the schedule shows her on leave for the next week."

"On leave? I didn't know about that?"

"That's what it says, man. You sure she didn't tell you?"

"No, at least I don't remember."

"Cory, while I have you on the phone I was curious how are you doing? Are you feeling okay?"

"I'm just really tired but I'll be okay. Thanks sir, I'll call back later and we'll talk."

"Okay, just try an stay in touch."

I hang up and toss the phone on the couch as I think back and try to remember if this was mentioned to me but I don't recall anything about her going on leave.

"On leave?" I ask myself again as I sit on the couch and pull the towel tighter around my arm.

Why would she go on leave and not tell me? I walk into the kitchen to get some juice and notice a note on the fridge. It's from Marie saying she went back home to California for a few days so I could relax and she took Katie with her so I could rest.

"What in the hell is going on?"

"Did I miss something? Have I been asleep for like two weeks or what?" I ask myself as I rub away the sweat that begins to form on my forehead.

Suddenly, my head begins to throb. I feel it pounding beneath my hand as I lose my balance and start to fall. I luckily catch myself on the edge of my couch with my other hand to remain on my feet. I become dizzy and my legs are weak, the sounds of faint voices begin to echo in my head. Male and female voices' just talking but it's too loud and stifled to make out. All I can identify is the pain that comes from them. I put my hands over my ears and squeeze my eyes shut, I try my hardest to block out the unrecognizable words and noises. I can feel my blood pulsate through my skull and force itself through my veins. The images in the room shake from the vibrations pushing through my head. As the voices and noises begin to fade away, the strength in my legs begin to return. I need to see a doctor, maybe even the lying doctor that released me yesterday. It's possible I may have a concussion or something. I'll have to deal with my wife and daughter once I can concentrate. But why would she just leave after what happened to me? The more I think about it the more my head and body aches. I'm not in the condition to focus on that at the moment.

I need my daughter and wife with me now more than ever. I begin walking back into my room and grab the closest clothes I can spot and head towards the front door. I leave my apartment and notice the sun is out but the light is soft, yet the faint light produced by the sun still pierce my eyes. The light burns and forces me to squint as I move down the stairwell. Surprisingly I notice my legs are numb. I can't feel the impact of the steps on my body and I start to slow down as it becomes more and more apparent. But the more I begin to notice their absence, I suddenly notice them returning. Like a small glitch the world forgot to add but corrected once realized.

I get in my truck and head towards the base to see my primary military doctor; it feels as if the trip is shorter than I remember; like I moved right down the street from the hospital. I vaguely remember seeing anything besides my parking lot and the base entrance. My mind seems to be skipping around.

I walk into the office and tell the receptionist that my head is pounding and that my arm has been bleeding and I just want to see someone. She takes down my information and I move into the waiting room. I lean back in the chair and just look at the people that litter the room. I wonder why they are here today. What could be wrong with them? After some time passes my name is called and I'm directed to the back, where I'm placed in a stranger's office surrounded by his achievements hanging on the wall staring back at me. The wall is covered with degrees and letters of thanks. I suppose this should lead me to believe that I'll be in good hands. As I sit down, the door opens behind me, I stand up as the doctor enters.

"Hello, please sit down and make yourself comfortable."

He tells me as he enters the room and makes his way around his desk while running his fingers across the top of his head. He tries to arrange the few strands of hair he has left to cover his forming bald spot. He looks across his desk at me with the excitement of a corpse as he extends his hand in the obligated manner we've all grown to accustom to. After a few shakes and nods he leans back in his huge leather chair. His uniform is old and disheveled but being a doctor in the military tends to make you look that way. I lean back and stare at him; we both sit awkwardly waiting for the other to start this uncomfortable conversation. It should be awkward for me but why is he so unreceptive?

5

TREATMENT

We stare at each other and then his eyes quickly widen as he finally breaks the silence with a deep breath.

"Well, Staff Sergeant Smith, umm…well I'm Dr. Masella, what seems to be the problem?"

"It's kind of strange sir; I'm not sure where to begin. I think I may have a concussion from yesterday. See, I got hit by a car……"

"Wait, you were hit by a car?" He interrupts with actual enthusiasm.

"Yes, yesterday, and now I get headaches and I hear pounding noises almost like voices. I just can't make them out."

Dr. Masella pulls out a pen and notebook and starts taking notes.

"Okay, well let's explore this. What happened exactly? How'd you get hit?" Dr. Masella asks as he crosses his legs and taps his pen to his glasses.

"I'm not really sure to tell you the truth. I mean I saw a girl walk in front of a speeding car outside of Wal-Mart and I pushed her out of the way. The car hit me and everything went black after that. I vaguely remember being in an ambulance then I woke up in a hospital room. But when I woke up I felt fine, just a little sore and tired. It felt fishy and I spoke with the doctor but he said I was fine. He informed me that the drugs the hospital gave me were making me feel better. I was pretty tired at the time so I really didn't ask much about it. He told me if I felt off to come back but I'd rather come here because I know I'd be seen faster and I'm sure I'd be asked to come here eventually anyway."

"Okay, so your head has been bothering you? Is that it?"
"Well it's not quite that simple. If I only had headaches then I wouldn't have come in today. First of all everything looks darker, like light is dull everywhere and this morning when I woke up my arm was bleeding for no reason. It was bleeding

where an IV would go but there are no marks from yesterday or anything."

"Interesting, let me see your arm."

He walks around the table and takes my arm.

"There are no holes or cuts. How did you see blood?"

He asks as he examines my arm turning it every way possible.

"I'm not sure, but there was blood and sharp little pains. It was rolling out from here."

"Was the blood new or did it seem old?"

I give him a bewildered look, "It was fresh, I saw it roll down my forearm and I touched it."

"Hmm, is there anything else going on in your life besides this?" He lets my arm go and moves back to his chair.

"Well I'm having some personal issues but that has nothing to do with this."

"Maybe it does. Maybe they're connected. What kind of issues are they?"

"I seriously doubt that my wife and I having minor issues would cause my arm to just bleed out of nowhere and the issues are not incredibly serious. She just kind of left out of nowhere to go on leave but I don't want to make it bigger than it may be. She may have told me but I just don't remember". I reply firmly.

"You know Cory I think you suffered what sounded like a traumatic experience and you seem a little stressed. My recommendation would be for you to go up stairs and talk to Capt. Daniels." He replies as he starts writing on his clip board.

"Capt. Daniels? Isn't he the mental health doctor?"

"Yes he is, is that a problem for you?" He answers as he stops writing and peels his eyes up towards me.

"You think this is all in my head?" I aggressively answer.

"Look Cory, I didn't say that. But I think we should look at all possible scenarios. I'll give you a referral slip and you can go see him, okay? Because I don't see anything wrong with you besides stress and before I prescribe you anything I want all the facts. It may be a slight concussion or more but you should speak with him before we go down that road."

I put my head down and start shaking it.

"Well let's wait a day or so just in case I start feeling better, would that be ok? I'd really prefer not going up stairs and speaking to him today. I'm just tired and want to rest."

"If you believe that would help I'll allow that." He nods his head in agreement.

"Well is there anything I can have for my headaches; is there something you recommend?"

"Just Excedrin or Advil will be fine for now."

I leave the doctor's office irritated. Here are the guys that are supposed to help you when you feel bad. Not refer you to someone else. As I enter my truck, the pain in my arm starts coming back. Wonderful, perfect timing, right after I leave the doctor's office.

I get in my truck and just sit there and wait for the pain to subside. A flaming sensation enters my lower back. My whole body starts to tingle and my legs go numb. I sit back in my car and try to work through the pain, my eyes tighten. I try to look around and notice the world seems to have changed. Everything seems old, yet new, like I've seen it all before but now in a new way. There is a new idea behind every old static item that fights its way into my view. I look at some of the buildings on base and the colors seem altered or not as detailed as they once were. Almost like looking at everything in a picture rather than actually being in its presence. Is this all really in my head or is there more to this puzzle than what my eyes are allowing me to see.

On my drive home I try calling Marie's cell phone but there is no answer. I leave her a message asking when she decided she was going on leave and why she didn't tell me. I told her I missed her and wanted her and Katie back so I didn't feel so alone and confused.

I hang up the phone and see a video rental store and decide to pull in and pick up a movie; it might calm me down so I can try to sort things out. I walk in and it's like being in a store filled with customers by myself. Almost as if I'm not even a part of their world or they are not a part of mine, they see me and we connect eyes but that's it. It's as if there is a secret everyone knows but me. I try to nod and smile at people as they pass by but no emotion is shown, no reactions. What's stranger than this is that they treat each other in the same manner, like their sole purpose is to walk around and look busy. I feel like I'm Jim Carrey in "The Truman Show". It's almost irritating; unless I'm beginning to over analyze my environment. I just shake my head and dismiss everyone and start walking down the aisles but nothing catches my eye. All the movies scream the same things, either plot less action flicks, drama movies with no depth, or the same seen it a thousand times college based spin off comedies. I decide to just leave and go home; I just want to go to bed. I pass a few fast food joints on the way home but I have no appetite. I start thinking and am almost shocked to recognize that I haven't eaten all day and I haven't been hungry once. Not one time have I felt hungry with all the mental rings I've jumped through; screw it I just want to go home. I enter my apartment and go straight into my room and fall on the bed. As I roll over I pray for a better tomorrow.

6

PAST RETURNS

My eyes open and I find myself less than two feet from the ceiling. I lean up quickly and notice I'm in my old bed in Florida where I grew up and I'm on the top bunk of my brother and I's old bunk beds. I sit there and begin to shake in fear. My eyes widen and intensify with panic as my hands begin to sweat. I hear sounds coming from under my bunk and I'm almost too petrified to look. I slowly lean over the rail and see my little brother jumping out of bed and running out of the room. He looks like he's seven but he should be twenty-six now. I shake my head and slide my hand onto my forehead and start massaging my temples.

"What the hell is going on?" I ask myself while I hold back the tears forming in my eyes.

I close my eyes again and take a deep breath, I look up and my room is exactly how I remembered it when I was a kid. If my brother is seven then I'd be ten.

The red toy chest on the far wall under the football curtains are the same as they were when I was little. The floor is still covered with the brown shag carpeting. I haven't lived here in fourteen-years, not since my parents were still married. Speaking of my parents, I hear them talking in the living room. I slowly get out of bed and peer out the door. I feel the shag carpet rise between my toes. I ease my way out and move down the hallway slowly, I slowly peer around the wall into this surreal twilight zone. As I enter the living room, my family is waiting for me. I stand in front of them shocked and speechless. My Mom and Dad are sitting next to each other, which is very unusual. My sister is on the love seat sitting across from me. This can't be; everyone is looking at me like I'm being sent to Iraq again. They look at me like I've been there this whole time. As if I've never groan up. I'm only ten years old? I'm so confused. They see me as their son who hasn't been to college; who doesn't have a kid, or a wife. They just see me as their son, like my whole life is still in front of me. They all get up and put their arms around me and squeeze tightly as they proceed to tell me they love and miss me. This is not my family, my family doesn't do this. This never happened even when I was ten, I disliked my brother growing up. We were rivals until we grew up and we never hugged one another.

"Mom? Dad? What's going on?" I ask while they are holding me but they don't pay my words any attention.

"Aww…I miss you baby please come back?" My Mom whispers to me as she buries her face into my shoulder.

"What are you talking about I'm right here. My question is how can this be?" I respond.

This can't be real! This isn't how my family is. This is more like how I wanted my family to be. We all loved each other but we've never been this affectionate. I get emotional and lost in the moment, I squeeze my arms around them and start to cry; I'm pulled out of my comfort zone and we all proceed to weep together.

"Mom, Dad, I don't know what's going on and I'm scared…" I force out while I shake and cry.

Then my eyes quickly open and I grab my chest. I roll out of bed and fall to the floor. I hit the floor hard but give the pain it causes no attention; I pull my knees toward my chest. My torso and body constrict and then tighten like a vice grip has been wrapped around me. It gets harder and harder to breathe and then the pain starts to subside as I roll over and my eyes water and my chest burns. My body starts shaking and the lights around me pulsates with every beat of my heart. The voices in my head come back and begin to torture me again. The noises split my head! That seems to be their sole purpose; I can almost feel the blood push into my skull as my body switches between hot and cold flashes. My hand feels really tight like its being squeezed by a giant. I can't close it, its cramped open. I feel as if the bones are being crushed within it by some outside force. Right when the pain becomes unbearable it loosens its grasp on me and I just lay on the floor shaking from whatever madness my body has inherited. I think of my wife Marie and my baby girl. I just want to see them; I just want to have them hold me. I want to hear my wife's sweet voice and see my daughter's beautiful little smile. Tears roll out of my eyes and I sob to myself. I try to compose myself and focus but I shake even more when I notice I'm back in my apartment in Texas. That dream felt so real but also emotionally brutal.

7

ANALYSIS

I force myself out of my bedroom and head towards the couch. I sit down and start thinking of everything that's happened in the last couple of days and how I got to this point. What really annoys me is I had so many friends and people that I thought cared for me but now, I feel deserted. I feel left out in this world. I have no friends to talk to and when I do work up the courage to call them I get the overwhelming feeling not to. Like if I do, I'll be talking to myself on the other line. They can't help me because I can't help myself. It's as if everyone has forgotten me and left me too deal with this on my own, but what is this? The confusion is driving me insane.

My mind feels twisted and frayed, but is it just from the accident? I decide to go on base and talk to the Mental Health Doctor with the referral slip given to me by Dr. Masella.

I grab the keys from the wall and walk outside my apartment. The sky is as black as night and rain is pouring down. I can barely feel the rain running down my face or even landing on me. I get in the truck, crank the engine and begin to back out of the driveway; I'm almost instantly at my destination. I walk into the hospital and the building is huge on the outside but it seems somehow small and catered to me on the inside. Nothing is as it was yesterday. Everyday objects have lost their natural detail and items scattered throughout the room have lost their meanings. I have developed some kind of tunnel vision in the outside world. My mind only focuses on what I need to see, everything else doesn't matter. People that I pass become more like moveable objects rather than other flesh and blood individuals. They may all look different but if they were all identical they would serve the same purpose, as if you're playing a video game with a scratched disk and a glitch in the game that rendered the looks and behaviors of every character the same. What's stranger than that is the fact that every day as I notice things changing, I care less and less. I walk up to the desk and say I need to see Capt. Daniels and that I was referred by Dr. Masella. I hand the receptionist my referral slip.

She sends me in before anyone else in the waiting room. Might as well; they look like they're just extras in a movie rather than being there for actual help.

I walk into the office and the Captain is sitting in his plush leather chair looking up at me.

"SSgt Wilson welcome. Please sit." He asks as he pulls out a pen and paper. "So what's going on son?"

I shake my head in an uninviting way, "Umm...well it's a long story but first I want to say with no disrespect to you, I don't feel like I need to be here. At least in the sense that, I know I'm not crazy; I don't have any mental problems in my background to put me in this chair and no one else in my family has mental issues that I know of. I'm just here because no one else seems to want to help me or know how to including myself."

"Well I'm not saying you should or shouldn't be here, let's just talk and see where that leads, okay? And you must remember that not everyone that comes here are crazy or anything like that. Sometimes people just need help dealing with things in a different way which I try to provide."

I take a deep breath and reply, "Okay, well let's get started then."

Capt. Daniels picks up his clip board and starts asking me basic questions about my past: where I grew up, what I liked doing as a kid, the basic psychology 101 questionnaire I guess. Then he asks me the hardest and most complex question to date:

"So what's been bothering you lately?"

"Well basically for the last few days my mind has been playing tricks on me."

"Hmm, that's interesting, how so?" He asks as his eyes widen and he starts chewing on the end of his pen.

"Ok, well I fall asleep for like a second and when I wake up, the clock shows 8:00am and….."

"Was your alarm set?" Capt. Daniels interrupts.

"No, I just wake up at 8am; I haven't been setting the alarm."

"Ok, go on."

"Well, it's hard to explain but it seems like whatever I think I need is there for me, except for friends and family, just my local environment. My days wiz by and when I feel sleepy, the day becomes dark and when I'm not, its day; my whole world is awkward and I guess unique. At least in my eyes anyway."

"Can you give me more examples? Those are a little hard to follow."

"Well for example normally driving to the hospital would have taken 15-20 minutes from my apartment but it seems like whatever I want is right around the corner; my mind is making things easier for me. I got in my car knowing I was coming here, then boom, I'm in the building; parked and everything. But at the same time my mind is losing details on other things as well. Like objects lose their meanings or pictures aren't as clear anymore. People look like inert objects, they are only there because they should be there, nothing seems real to me anymore. The environment and my life have no detail, I guess. I have tunnel vision and only care about what I need. It's hard to explain"

"SSgt Wilson, this is a little confusing and I can't totally comprehend what you're saying."

Capt. Daniels puts the clipboard down and stares at me as if I were a human Rubik's cube.

"Do you feel depressed? Is family life okay for you?"

"I'm getting depressed about this; my family life is weird right now, and it seems like that's where you and everyone else want to pawn this off but it's not my family."

"Well why not? Your paperwork says you're married, if you're not happy that might have a bearing on this?"

"Ok, let me explain this to you doc, I am married, my wife took my daughter and went on leave, out of nowhere or at least I don't remember being told about it. This made me furious, but as time went on I feel like it was easier for me to be without them. But that makes no sense. I love them both more than anything, they are all I care about and all I need in life. The weird thing is, now that they're gone, I think that might be a good thing for me right now. I don't know what's wrong with me but it's easier without them here. I've tried calling but lately I've been slacking off because in my head I know they're fine. I just feel like if they were around this issue I'm dealing with would be way harder for me. Every day I lay down to sleep and when I wake up I notice that my life has deteriorated more and more and I'm beginning to care less and less."

"Have you tried calling your parents about this or do you ever feel like giving up?"

"I do think about my friends and family all the time but when I talk to them I really feel like I'm just talking to myself. Even now talking to you, you're asking me questions that I would ask myself, and it's frustrating."

"Well…"

I cut him off and continue my rant.

"Let me ask you this doc. Why does my arm randomly bleed?" I lean in closer to him.

"Well I……."

I cut him off again, "why do I get constant throbbing headaches and hear voices screeching under my skull? Echoes that pound in my head like war drums? Why do I randomly get woozy and my chest starts to hurt and I feel like vomiting out of nowhere, why?"

"Umm…I don't know, that's….."

My voice deepens, "That's right, you don't know because I don't know, and you're about as useful as I am trying to solve this. The longer I'm here the more time I feel like I'm wasting. I just want to go home. I think I just figured this entire thing out." I get out of the chair and head for the door.

"Cory, we're not done, you have a lot of emotions flowing through you right now and we need to talk. So please take a seat. I want to hear what you think you have figured out." He anxiously asks.

"I figured out that only I can help myself. You can't help me. Just let me come back tomorrow doc. I can't deal with this right now I just want to relax." I ask with the door knob in my hand.

"SSgt Wilson, if you calm down then I'll consider it okay, just relax and let's make an appointment. Please see my nurse when you leave and if you start to feel worse then call me, ok? I'm not going to let you leave without knowing you're okay."

I take a deep breath and calm down. "Yes, I'm better now, I'm sorry. I guess I just needed to vent and let off some steam. I haven't been getting a lot of sleep lately and I'm not going to do anything stupid. So you don't have to worry about that."

"Do you promise to call me if something comes up? And I'm going to have my nurse call you tomorrow to see how you're doing okay."

"I will and that's fine." I nod back at him.

A false promise, I don't need someone to tell me my mind is torn apart, I can see that myself. I just need to unwind and calm down. I just want to go home. That's the only place I feel somewhat at peace.

8

WRECKED

I leave the doctor's office and enter the pouring rain. I refuse to cover my head, my eyes close tightly. I start feeling sharp pains in my head as the annoying voices try to penetrate my thoughts; I shake them off trying and try to avoid the possible headache. I'm tired of them annoying me so I'm just going to try to suck it up and ignore them the best I can. I get into my truck and slam the door behind me; I catch a glance at myself in the mirror. My eyes look almost blood shot and my lip is quivering with the rage inside me that is beginning to boil over. I'm pissed from the doctors' lack of help and by having to hear the same questions over and over again. I'm tired of talking about this; I just want it to stop. I pull my truck out of the parking lot and squeal tires as I exit the base. I squeeze the wheel tightly while I drive. My aggression increases and I slam my head back into the head rest and scream as loud as I can as I yank on the wheel!

All of a sudden I start to feel tired, my eye lids feel heavy; I just need to go home and lie down. I roll my shoulders and shake my head to wake up but my eyelids continue to close. I shake my head again and try to sit up taller in my seat. I decide to turn the radio on, music should help keep me awake, but as I start pressing the buttons, a loud horn begins screaming in front of me. I'm shocked by the noise and I quickly look up to see that I've drifted into oncoming traffic. The horn blares again from a huge black pick-up truck as I try to turn the wheel quickly back into my lane. But it's too late, our vehicles collide. It happens so fast I can't avoid it. My front driver's side hits theirs, but I don't feel the impact, not until I'm almost half way through his truck. Our eyes lock onto each others; terror grips both of us and time seems to slow down. Our eyes are pulled apart from the force tearing into both of our bodies. Then my truck jumps and starts to roll and flip across the road towards a grassy ditch. Glass starts piercing my skin and the flesh begins to tear off my body, thunderous noises from metal to gravel enter the air as my trucks interior shrinks and squeezes on top of me.

The sound of glass breaking fills the air. I start to think that I'm going to die inside this truck. Then on the third turn, my seat belt snaps off and I'm thrown through the battered front window. I see images in quick rolling flashes and hear screeching noises as rain starts hitting the ground. My body collides with the ground and I slide through the wet grass onto my stomach. I slowly open my eyes and see that my face is in a mud puddle; bubbles appear on the water from beneath my mouth, they grow and pop with every breath I take. Warm strands run down my face and I can see blood dripping from my head onto my arms. Lacerations going up and down my arms begin blending into the dirty water. I try to push myself to my knees and amazingly I can. Glass shards are painfully placed throughout my body. I finally decide to look up and see the extent of damage I've caused with my careless driving. But oddly I see and hear nothing, just faltering silence. No other cars or people. I close my eyes real tight and pull my head up towards the sky as I let the water run down my face. I open my eyes and look back down to see no more cuts on my arms, no more tears on my skin. The glass is gone, I start shaking in fear and as I look around I see my apartment. I stand up and feel fine. There is no more rain, no cars in traffic, and no wreck whatsoever. I just hit a truck leaving base where is it? Is the driver ok? Was anyone injured? I see my truck parked in my apartments designated spot. I start weeping because now I know I'm losing my mind.

I start walking towards my apartment and keep pulling on my dry shirt trying to get past this anxiety. I take a long, deep breath as fear grips my body and I notice that I'm lost in my own world. I couldn't have dreamt the wreck, because I was just lying in the mud right outside the base entrance. How did I get here? Nothing makes sense to me anymore. If the wreck didn't happen, did my trip to the doctor? I know this had to have happened or did it?

9

END IS NEAR

I wake up feeling sicker than I have ever felt before, like after a long night of binge drinking. My body feels beaten and my eyes carry images across the room. Everything I see blurs from object to object and it only exacerbates my nausea. I feel my heart pounding through my body and the beats echo in my head. I pull in half a breath then my chest collapses. The voices in my head are louder than normal and they won't stop. My skull is throbbing in unison with every heart beat that pumps through my body. I put my moist palms on my head and the sweat feels cool and soothing against my hot skin. My eyes water as I turn over in my bed and glance at the clock, 8:00am. What other time did I expect? My life has been defaulted to start at 8:00am. I feel so weak, I pull myself to my feet and almost fall back on the bed but I catch myself on the bed post. My legs quiver and shake like wet noodles; soreness and infirmity flood my body and the manner is unrelenting. There are no medicines for what I have.

Today everything's dark, not dim or faint, just dark. Unlike the past few days when the world had more life and color, now it's bland and unnervingly motionless. I finally get my legs controlled under me and slowly stumble into the closet. There's an antique case on the top shelf next to my gym bag. This case is the only thing in the closet my eyes can put color or focus on. I extend my arms and pull the case down. I take a deep breath as I open the case to see the 9mm that was given to me by my uncle on my last birthday. I look at it for a moment and stare at my reflection mirror off the smooth silver finish. My blue eyes seem to burn into the steel. I grab the clip as the gun begins to blur in front of me as I struggle to load it, the cold steel feels comforting and welcome in my hands. I push in the clip and hear the click whisper "it's okay"; I take another deep breath as I slowly slide a round into the chamber. I do it slowly so I can watch the bullet move into position before I slide the top back. I hold it at my side like an assassin while walking through the hallway and into the living room. I notice only static items that clutter my house. The family portraits are blank. The picture frames hold only images my mind will allow me to see. The whole room revolves around me like a cold tomb rather than a warm cozy home. I sit on the couch and lean back, whimpering with pain and anger. Tunnel vision and distant memories flood my consciousness. I remember myself watching television with my mother and sister, and playing catch with my brother and father. Old memories that I wish I could relive begin tormenting me. The inside of my eyelids reveal the first time I saw my beautiful wife. I was sitting in a chair at work laughing with a friend when she walked in front of us and caught my eye and her image never let me go. Then our wedding day starts to slowly playback in my mind. I see my daughter's birth and the doctors handing her to me. As I held her little hand and looked at my wife, I hoped to be the father and husband they deserved. My chest begins to constrict causing a chain reaction of pain that begins to dart down my body as the voices in my head get louder and more prominent. They're driving me mad! Thunderous words that I can't make out. All I get from them are mind splitting headaches that irritate every fiber of my being. All my thoughts and memories begin to blend together and nothing makes sense anymore. Every word chimed in my head causes my vision to shake and shutter. I should call someone for help but who? I already know that everyone I'd call would just annoy me. They'll all give me answers that I already have; they'll ask questions that I've already asked. I want to get up and move on with my life but life seems so hard right now and this pain is unbearable. I can't move past this and it just keeps getting worse. My worlds falling apart, my very fabric of existence is deteriorating with every breathe I take. I don't want an easy way out. I'm a soldier, a husband, a father, and a friend to a world that's left me behind. A world that's given up on me; how things got so bad so quickly, I can't explain and I fear I'll never know. I look down at the gun and admire the silvery finish as its sight continues to calm me. I look around and feel like a stranger in my own home. I reluctantly pull the gun under my chin and I feel a tear roll down my left cheek as my head follows it to the floor. The room feels like its spinning around me. My vision blurs and everything begins to fade away. Total silence enters the room and finally into my head. The relief is only temporary. The voices return and they've grown stronger than ever. They're yelling at me but why? Why do they constantly torment me?

Like clockwork, the constrictions tear through my body and shiver down my spine. Like chills from being cold but they brought a fire that flows through my veins and throughout my body. My body quivers in pain as I move my head back up; I'm out of my home now and see my daughter running towards me smiling with my beautiful wife close behind her. She's running in a meadow pushing through the grass and bright yellow daises, she smiles at me as the sun reflects off her perfect little face. Her little hazel eyes are the sharpest color in this memory. I barely feel the tears continue to roll down my face while I come to terms with the fact that this unclear, but understandable image will be the last time I see them. My girls, the loves of my life.

How do you fall asleep and wake up to such a twisted hell? A place where everyone and everything plays tricks on you, a place where you can't trust anything you see, think, or feel. A twilight zone so surreal you feel like you've awakened in a dream that's actually a reality. I will never kill myself; I've said it a million times. Suicide is never the right answer to any question life brings. My thoughts deepen as I envision kneeling down and hugging my daughter. My wife smiles and places her arms around us. This to me won't be suicide; it'll be a release. I slide my finger onto the trigger and start to squeeze, I can hear the hammer pull back with a light whisper: "it's okay" and my ears focus on that sound. Then the hammer slams back into the gun. The room jumps quickly, and then everything goes black.

10

DISCOVERY

A doctor leaves the hospital room with his head down cleaning off his glasses with the bottom of his white coat. As he slowly raises his head and puts the glasses back on, he raises his right hand and lays it on Marie's shoulder. She looks at him with tears rolling down her cheeks.

"It's over now, I'm sorry. He's at peace now." He says with a soft voice.

"Can I go in and see him?" She mumbles as she wipes her face and tries to compose herself. Her body starts to tremble violently.

"Yes, of course." He puts his hand on her shoulder and walks her through the door into the large white room.

Marie sees her husband lying motionless on a hospital bed staring up at the ceiling with wet lines on his cheeks where the tears were rolling down his face. Two nurses are unplugging machines from him and one slides her hand down his face closing his lifeless eyes. They hear Marie whimpering behind them and stop. They back away as she moves toward Cory.

"I can't believe this happened!" Marie says as she walks closer.

"He did a brave thing Mrs. Smith, you should be proud. These situations are never easy." The doctor tries to comfort her with his gentle words.

Marie leans over and drapes her body across Cory's chest as she begins to weep uncontrollably. The nurses work around her to remove the IVs out of his arms while blood starts running down his forearms into his hands.

"I just thought that all the time we spent talking to him and all the time his family spoke to him would help. Maybe bring him out of this, it would wake him up you know?"

She tells the doctor as she squeezes her arms around Cory's still warm body.

"Look Mrs. Smith, I've seen individuals in your husband's position many times and sometimes it does help to talk to them but then sometimes the words just can't get through. Would you like me to tell his family outside or do wish to do that?"

"No, I will. I think they should hear it from me."

Marie leans up and tries to wipe the continuous flow of tears from her face. She let's go of her husband's hand and slowly moves back towards the door. It's hard for her to take her eyes off of him as she walks out. She makes her way down the hall to the waiting room where the rest of the have been patiently waiting.

As she enters the room, the expression on her face says more than her words ever could. Cory's father, Lewis, stands up and carries his son's three year old daughter out of the room. His lip starts to quiver while Katie lowers her head down onto his shoulder crying for Daddy to please wake up. Marie's mother walks over and puts her arms around her. Then Cory's mother Monica hugs his sister. Marie's mother walks outside and takes Katie from Lewis. As Lewis walks back into the room Marie takes his hand and leads him and Cory's mother into the room where their son is lying. As they enter they see Cory with bandages still wrapped around his head and his chest red and exposed where the medical staff have been giving him shocks with the defibrillator. They walk up to their son and kiss him on the forehead. The doctor comes in and stops at the end of the bed and lets out a deep sigh.

"I'm very sorry for your loss; I assure you we did everything we could. He was just tired and may have given up; his strength had to be wearing thin. But you have to realize some people come out of comas and some do not." The doctor says with a soft voice.

"Do you think he felt any pain over the last few days?" Monica asks as she turns to him.

The doctor clears his throat and replies:

"Ma'am, I've been around a lot of patients that have come out of comas after being under for years and some have said they heard everything that their friends and family said to them. Others say that they heard nothing. The mind is a magnificent organ. For all we know he could've been awake in his mind this whole time living very happily. That's at least what I like to believe and I hope you see it that way as well, for Cory to be in his mind at peace with good memories and the voice of his loving family. All we know now is that he's at peace."

Lewis gives his son one last quick kiss on the head and squeezes his dead hand then walks out not saying a word to anyone. The doctor follows him with his eyes while he walks out.

Monica turns to address the doctor, "Thanks for all you tried to do for my son. It's sad, you hear about people in comas all the time but you would just never believe someone in your family, especially one of your children would ever be in one." She hugs Marie and they begin to cry.

It's raining at the funeral but no one seems to notice as the water rolls off the overhang made by the canopy. After the sermon, the flag folding begins. It's presented to Marie and then the playing of taps begin. Once the music stops, everyone lines up to pay their final respects. The first person in line to drop a white rose in Cory's grave is Jessica. The little girl Cory saved from the speeding car.

TORRE ODELL

AUTHOR COMMENTS

I understand this story is not well written and that was ironically the point. I wanted the story to flow in and out like a wave of consciousness, for the reader to feel like they are somewhat between a dream and reality. The idea was to create a sense of confusion and leave the perception of the story to be rather unnerving. The story is erratic like the mind of the main character. The lack of detail was concurrent with the detail his mind provided. Of course with the lack of detail and mental skips, the story provides less information when it should provide more.

The idea for "Psyche" came to me while stationed at Enrique Soto Cano, Air Base, Honduras. When you're in the military and you get an assignment to Central America, you are prescribed Malaria pills which you take before you arrive the country. Malaria pills have many side effects such as nausea, headaches, and even vivid dreams. The only issue I encountered was the vivid dreams. One night I had a dream almost exactly like the novel. My mind played tricks on me and caused me to suffer. I remember trying to wake up but when I did, it was just a new day within the same dream. When I finally woke up I started writing down everything I could remember. I played with the idea for a few years and then decided to see if I could actually get it published. Which led us to this point.

TORRE ODELL

ABOUT THE AUTHOR

Torre Odell, Military Training Manager / Author, has been writing short stories and comedy scripts for many years but never tried to publish until now. His creative abilities started to overwhelm him after he enlisted in the military. While stationed in Texas he performed at comedy clubs in Addison and Dallas as much as he could. He garnered excellent reviews and was written about in a local newspaper. Although due to his military obligations he had to stop performing. He then started committing his free time to writing and higher education. This is his first novel.

Education:

AS Information Systems – Community College of the Air Force, 2010

BA Social & Criminal Justice – Ashford University, 2009

MS Leadership & Information Technology – Duquesne University, 2011

Affiliations:

Graduate and Professional Counsel (Duquesne University)

Golden Key International Honour Society

TORRE ODELL

Years of Dorin

(Chapter one: Sample)

Torre Odell

1

DEADLY NIGHT

It's strange, I'm almost 200 years old but I remember this year better than any other. I've spoken with many people who can't even remember events that happened in their lives last week and when you've lived as long as I have it becomes hard to remember days and dates but you remember the years, at least I do…in horrific flashes. The year was 1817…

It was a cold night in Romania, I don't know what province anymore or if I ever did. I do remember being woken up by screams and the smell of smoke. I got out of bed and ran out of my small dark room along with my two younger brothers. My older sister Ada was guarding the front door in the living room. She huddled us all together as we entered the room. I noticed my mother and father were missing during this madness. I could see people running by our small home through the small cracks on our front door.

Smoke started entering the room as fire started to light up the roof. Ada, rushed us all outside and we saw horsemen riding through the village throwing flaming sticks on our homes. The villagers were trying to fight these invaders off but were unsuccessful. Our village was made up of mainly farmers, no warriors or soldiers. We just stood there while the men began to dismount their horses and proceed to slaughter everyone they came in contact with. My older sister Ada stood in front of us for protection but none of us moved. We were frozen by fear. I tried to look through the smoke and chaos for my parents but I couldn't find them. I remember wanting my father there to protect us. Through the smoke my eyes finally connected with my mother and she began to run towards us. She was within 10 feet of us before an explosion of blood came up from behind her head as her eyes widened and her body fell violently upon the cold snow. An axe was lodged into the back of her skull. Her body began to shake and move towards us then slowly stopped. My sister screamed as my mother's blood rolled down the hill and under our feet. I just stood in the snow and watched the steam rise from the wound on her head. My brothers and sister began crying in the snow as our world burned around us. We didn't know what to do or where to go. I didn't cry. I don't know if it's from fear or shock but I know I didn't cry. The attention my siblings brought from their weeping wasn't good. Within seconds of my mother's death I heard snow crunching beside us and as I turned I saw a huge figure approach us. Out of fear and instinct I grabbed a sword that was lying near our front door on top of a corpse and tried to protect what's left of my family. With a wild swing I stab the man quickly in his left thigh. He lets out a deep scream then quickly disarms me with a quick left hook to my head. The impact throws me against my front door and a high ringing pierces my skull and my whole body trembles in pain. The cold snow feels like a blanket of comfort when I landed on it. Everything goes black.

When I finally wake up I find myself tied to ever other kid in my village that wasn't killed in the chaos. My face was throbbing and I could feel thick dried blood on my face. My right eye was half closed and throbbing. I quickly scanned the children until I found my two brothers a few feet away from me which provided a little comfort. However the rest of the sights I wish I could forget. I wish I could skip that part in this story but I feel it would be an injustice to do so. Dead bodies were littered around us and two huge fires were burning. One fire was for cremating the dead bodies. The other was reserved for a more horrific use. All the girls and babies were being thrown into it. Dead or alive it didn't seem to matter. If the girls were old enough or strong enough to fight their way out they'd be killed then thrown back in. This happened in front of us like we weren't even there. The men from my village were already dead. I noticed only a few young girls, probably between the ages of 14-20, who were being salvaged. They were being tied up and moved out of the village, but for what purpose I didn't know.

Kids weren't crying or screaming due to being in shock. You may hear a whimper now and then but nothing more. I couldn't see my sister anywhere but I prayed she was one of the lucky ones saved. I looked over at my brothers and just knew death was coming. The tears finally began to come but as I started to break down, I heard a voice start to address us. The voice was old and deep but very strong.

"Your lives have been spared for a reason. This reason is more important then you or the loved one's you once had. You have been put on fates door step and a great opportunity awaits you. However all of you will not survive."

As he finishes the sentence select kids were pulled out of the lines.

"Right now I'm having the weaker or unfit pulled out of the group. They will be killed and if you don't perform appropriately you will be killed as well. I only want the best!"

I'm grabbed and thrown out of line with all the other so called unfit kids. I didn't fight nor did I care. I was happy for death at this point. I lose my breath when I see my 5 year old brother Luca next to me. I grab him and pull him close. I look up and see that my 8 year old brother Diamante was left in line. Being 10 and the oldest I knew that protecting them was up to me but I didn't know how. I was too small and too weak. It was hard to concentrate with all the confusion taking place but I started to hear death again. I looked over and saw these young boys being pulled up and having either their necks slit or they were just stabbed in the back. As I noticed this horrific site my little brother Luca was snatched out of my hands and dropped by my feet with blood beginning to cover his shirt, the blood was running out of his neck as his eyes glazed over then closed. My eyes opened to full capacity as I lost my breath. A huge hand grabs my head and squeezes my hair tightly as my head yanks back to expose my neck. I look up and saw a huge figure over me with a pale face, dark eyes, and pointed K9s. This was the first time I saw any of their faces. I felt a cold sticky blade touch my neck as I looked into his hateful eyes and then I heard a faint scream "MARCEL STOP!"

It was the old deep voice from earlier. As he walked up he told his other men to continue but not the one holding me. He stopped next to my attacker and began whispering to him.

"Marcel, why do you choose to kill this boy? He doesn't look weak just thin like many of the others."

Marcel answers with a scratchy voice filled with bass, "Forgive me Lord, it's payback, this boy stabbed me earlier. I see him as a trouble maker. We should eliminate him now and save the trouble."

"Did he now? Well I think we can salvage this boy. His ability to protect and quickly react may become useful if directed appropriately. Sheath your blade Marcel and put him back in line."

"Yes, Oxodus." The big man reluctantly agrees.

He releases my hair and pushes me onto the snow. My head still hurts from his tight grip. As my head falls into the snow my eyes instantly goes back to my little brother's body. I put my hand on Luca's motionless foot and move towards him but my face hits the icy snow. It's not cold...my face lands in a puddle of blood created by my little brother. I hear a deep scratchy voice into my ear with a cold breath on my neck as I stare into the red snow.

"Don't worry. You'll be dead like him soon enough, I promise, you won't live long slim. Now get back in line before that blood becomes your own."

I'm tied back into line with the remaining kids as I stare at Luca's body. I quickly look around and catch eyes with Diamante but he looks away. We're marched miles out of our village. As the night begins to end our captors were relieved by new soldiers. They dressed in black and were less imposing. I saw them talking but I couldn't make out their words. These new soldiers look and act normal and are clearly intimidated by their counterparts. They gather us together and make us march into a nearby forest. All we get to eat is small pieces of bread and a tiny amount of water. This is normally given to us during the day. Our nightly captors normally don't give us anything. Every night more kids are brought and tied to the group. Sometimes we'd be left outside a village for an entire day with only a few guards to watch us as more kids are captured each night. We'd hear the screams all night then be stuck with the stench of death all day. A lot of kids would throw up but over time the smell became less and less bothersome. The teenage girls that were taken were held away from us. We could always barely see them but when we were able to catch a glimpse of their group it would be smaller every morning. Or it would look a lot different due to the influx of new girls after a village was taken. These devil men of the night were odd to me. I would never see them eat and on a lucky day they'd just throw us dead animals and water sacks. The animals thrown to us never had blood, they were all bled dry. There was never enough food for all of us so many kids would die. They'd die from either lack of food and water or they'd be killed trying to get it. Speed became a necessity and so did silence. If you spoke you'd be punished. You speak when spoken to and those opportunities were rare. It's hard to ration out food and water in those conditions. Diamante and I looked at each other now and then but we didn't speak or even try. As long as I saw him every day I felt somewhat reassured. He may be all I have left. I didn't want the guards to know we were related. In fear of them using that to their advantage and hurting us even more in the future.

One thing we had in common with our day guards was fear. We as kids and prisoners were scared of everything but these men seemed scared of the night soldiers and us, not a physical danger from us but a fear of one of us actually escaping. No one dared to talk or even try to escape. Fear took our freedom. We were told if we tried to escape we'd be killed and so would the closest five kids to us. This may or may not have been a bluff but no one wanted to test it. The days were long and cold. We just walked everywhere. As kids died off we'd steal their clothes to help stay warm. The nights were lonely and freezing. If you died you were cut from the group and left. If you were sick they'd kill you in fear you'd get others sick. No one knew where we were marching too but none of us were in a hurry to get there. At night when the evil soldiers would return they'd taunt us along with the men who guarded us. They were so unusual, very pale and arrogant. We never saw them eat which I always looked for. Until I saw what happened to Ada...

TORRE ODELL

Thanks for Reading!